The Twelve Days Of Christmas

Published 1993 by
Treehouse Children's Books Ltd.,
8 North Road, Wells, Somerset BA5 2TJ.
Copyright © 1993 Treehouse Children's Books Ltd.
Illustrations copyright © 1993 John Blackman.
All rights reserved. Printed in Hong Kong.
ISBN 1-85576-139-4

The Twelve Days Of Christmas

A picture book with flaps by
John Blackman

TREEHOUSE

The first day of Christmas my true love sent to me ...

and a ...

The third day of Christmas my true love sent to me ...

and a ...

The fourth day of Christmas my true love sent to me ...

and a ...

The fifth day of Christmas my true love sent to me ...

and a ...

The tenth day of Christmas my true love sent to me ...

and a ...

The eleventh day of Christmas my true love sent to me ...

and a ...

The twelfth day of Christmas my true love sent to me ...

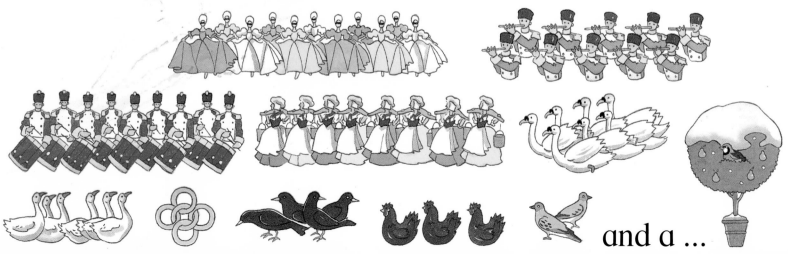

and a ...

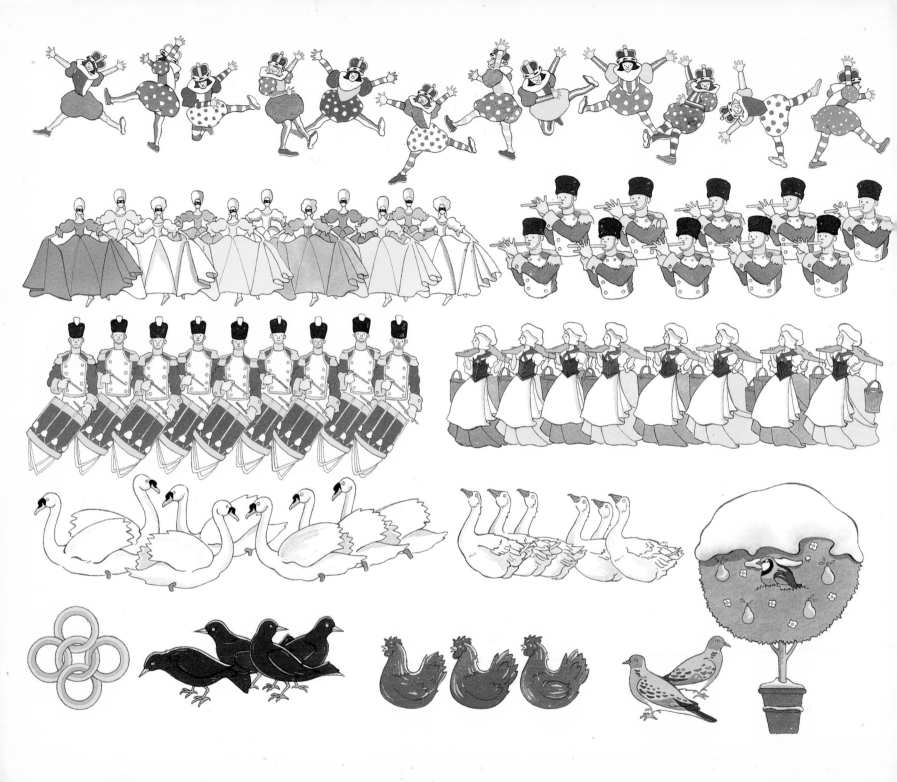